Can you use a
birthday wish
to wish

for a genie?

Enjoy!

M Stehly

To Bryndon, Cale, and Maritsa,
my birthday wishes come true.
—M. F.

To Lloyd, Elliott, Fraser, and Cameron.
The boys with the funniest minds.
—M. L.

STERLING CHILDREN'S BOOKS
New York

An Imprint of Sterling Publishing Co., Inc.
1166 Avenue of the Americas
New York, NY 10036

ISBN 978-1-4549-2233-9

Distributed in Canada by Sterling Publishing Co., Inc.
c/o Canadian Manda Group, 664 Annette Street
Toronto, Ontario M6S 2C8, Canada
Distributed in the United Kingdom by GMC Distribution Services
Castle Place, 166 High Street, Lewes, East Sussex BN7 1XU, England
Distributed in Australia by NewSouth Books
45 Beach Street, Coogee, NSW 2034, Australia

For information about custom editions, special sales, and premium and corporate purchases,
please contact Sterling Special Sales at 800-805-5489 or specialsales@sterlingpublishing.com.

Manufactured in China

Lot #:
2 4 6 8 10 9 7 5 3 1
11/18

sterlingpublishing.com

Design by Ryan Thomann
The artwork for this book was created digitally.

This is NOT a Dragon Party

by Mike Flaherty · illustrated by Maxime Lebrun

STERLING CHILDREN'S BOOKS
New York

I **knew** I should have hidden the phone from that dragon.

Now my birthday is ruined by a crazy dragon pool party, an **All-Out Dragon Bash**.

Sound awesome?
It's not.

All-Out Dragon Bashes are not as fun as they sound . . .
unless you are a dragon.

Rowdy, roaring dragons are splashing water everywhere.
My diving board is charred by fiery dragon breath.

And dragons doing cannonballs
have soaked my cat.

This dreadful dragon pool party must be stopped.

And I know **just** who can help me. . . .

I should have hidden the karaoke machine from those knights.

I'M IN LOVE WITH THE SHIELD OF YOURS

They didn't take care of my dragon party problem,

so now my house is packed with a crazy dragon pool party and a raucous karaoke festival, an **Up-All-Knight Shindig**.

Sound amazing?
It's not.

Up-All-Knight Shindigs are not as fun as they sound . . . unless you are a knight.

Clamorous crooning has cracked my glasses.

The air lute competition got a little out of hand.

And my cat is yowling along, too. She has a terrible singing voice.

This awful karaoke festival
must be stopped.

And I know
just who can
help me. . . .

I should have locked
my sister's bedroom door.

These ogres were supposed to help me
with my knight problem (they didn't).

Now my house is crowded with a crazy dragon pool party, a raucous karaoke festival, *and* an unruly ogre tea party, a **Tea and Crumpets Rumpus**.

Sound delightful?
It's not.

Tea and Crumpets Rumpuses are not as fun as they sound . . .
unless you are an ogre . . . or a princess . . . or an ogre princess.

My chairs are in splinters thanks to giant ogre butts.

Hungry, hungry
ogres devoured
all of my snacks.

And my cat hates wearing twinkling
tiaras. At least I think she does.

This horrible ogre tea party must be stopped.

But I don't know **who** can help me.

I guess it's up to **me** to save this birthday.

No more dragons!

No more knights!

Now, maybe I can
enjoy my birthday.

Is anyone going to sing "Happy Birthday"?

Anyone?

Ugh . . . **this boring birthday party must be stopped.**

And I think I know **just** what to wish for. . . .

Now my house is crawling with dragons, packed with knights, **and** crowded with ogres, and we're all throwing a **crazy, raucous, unruly** *birthday party.* Sound fantastic?